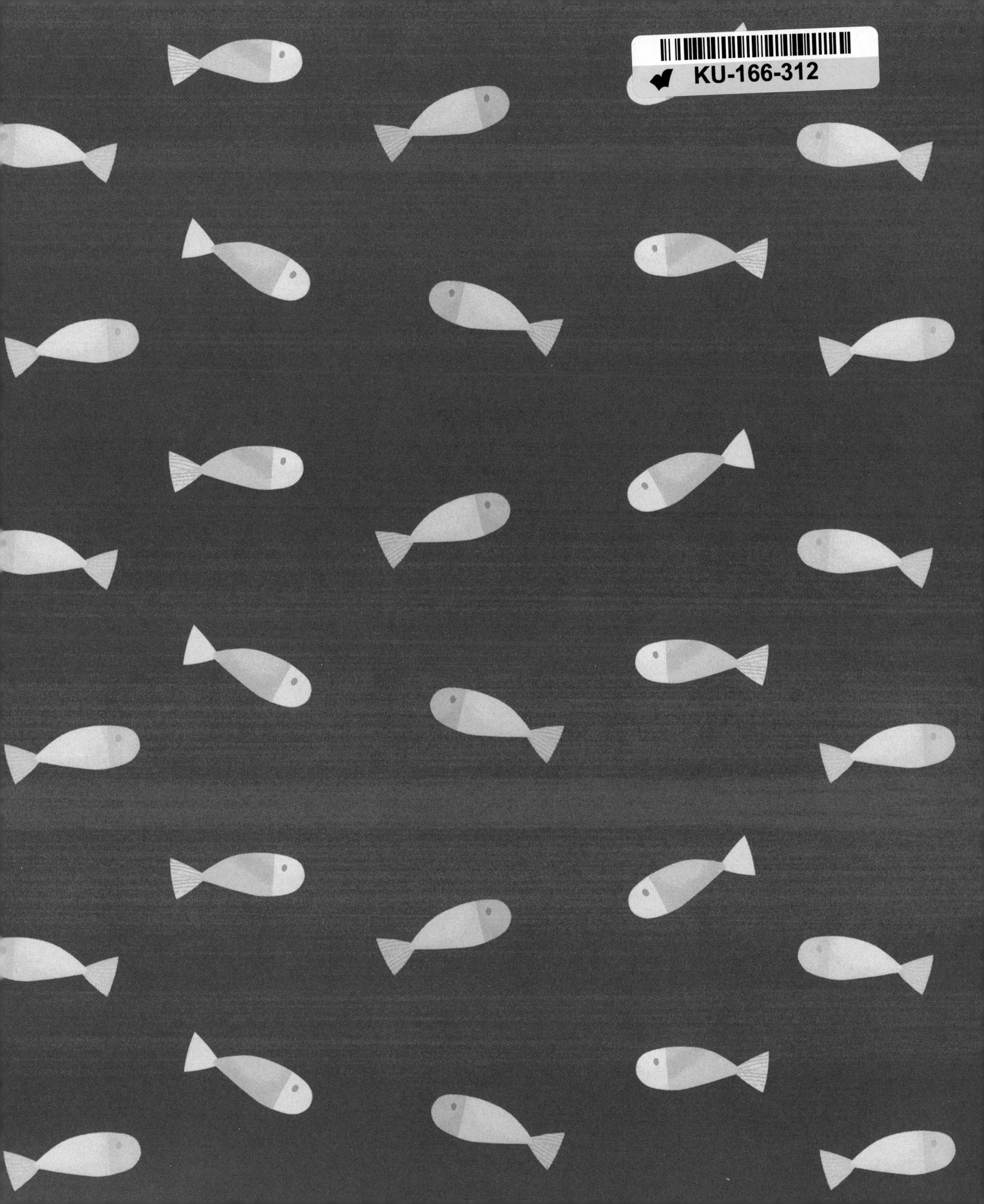
KU-166-312

Politeness for Penguins

Designed by Tabitha Blore
Edited by Lesley Sims
Design Manager: Nicola Butler

Usborne House, 83-85 Saffron Hill,
London EC1N 8RT, England

First published in 2022 usborne.com © 2022 Usborne Publishing Ltd. UE. All rights reserved. No part of this publication may be reproduced, stored in a retrieval system or transmitted in any form or by any means without the prior permission of the publisher. The name Usborne and the Balloon logo are Trade Marks of Usborne Publishing Ltd.

Politeness for Penguins

Zanna Davidson

Illustrated by
Duncan Beedie

This is **Little Waddlington** – a town just by the sea.
It looks so sweet and charming, as pretty as can be...

But it's full of **naughty** penguins with a **DREADFUL** attitude!

They're **squawky!**

They're **smelly!**

They are really very **rude!**

Meet the **hurly-burly** gentoos,
always in a rush,

shoving!

braying!

bumping!

as they **hurry** for the bus.

The rockhoppers are arguing. They love to interrupt.

While the chinstraps barge around, being **snappy** and **abrupt**.

Here come the macaronis. They're marching in to dine.
But when tummies start to **rumble**...

...they soon **tumble** out of line.

They have **no** table manners.
They **gobble** and they **crunch**.

The floor tells a sorry story of what they had for lunch.

As for the little penguins –
they **never** seem to learn.

So do you think these penguins
could **ever** change their ways?

It doesn't look too hopeful,
but then, one **breezy** day...

Faster than a hurricane,
the news whizzes round.

The Emperor is coming
on a special ROYAL MISSION!

He's here to find the winner
of the BEST TOWN COMPETITION.

The lucky town that wins this
will get its GREATEST wish...

...a whole year's FREE supply
of fresh and scrumptious fish!

Everyone's excited. Penguin flippers start to flap.
Eyes are out on stalks. Beaks go *clack-clack-clack*.
I'm sure that we can win!
We'll tidy up our streets.
We'll dust and clean and polish!
And make a YUMMY feast!

The Emperor comes tomorrow
so we're going to have to hurry...

"No! WAIT!" cries a gentoo.
"I've a dreadful, awful worry."

If we want to win the contest,
will we need to be polite?

"Oh no," groans a rockhopper.
"I think that gentoo's right."

"No matter," says a chinstrap,
"for I know just where to look.
Buried in the library is a dusty manners book."

"There's quite a lot to get through!
Here's all we need to know. Is everybody listening?

Ready... get set... GO!"

"Always say excuse me if you bump or burp or..."

"Don't interrupt – just **LISTEN.**

Look **others** in the **eye.**

Even if you're **bored**, don't fidget, yawn or sigh.

It's kind to hold doors open. It's polite to wipe your feet.

Don't rush or barge or push
or drop litter on the street.

Remember to take turns.
It's a lovely thing to share...

...from toys to food to clothes, to giving up your chair."

"At mealtimes, sit down nicely.
Don't try to eat **and** talk.

No feeding with your flippers!
Use a **knife and fork!**

It's good to think of others,
so even if the **fish**…

...is the one you love the most, please leave some on the dish!

And last but so important, don't forget to smile.

Then you'll be a perfect penguin...

with your own pizzazz and style."

The penguins try so hard...

...all through the day and night.

Then in the early morning,
a **big boat** comes ashore.

The Emperor gives a sigh, and swaggers through the crowd.
His beak is up, his tummy out – he looks extremely proud.

But the Emperor simply snorts. He shakes his silky head.
"Don't come too close, you peasants! You smell like fish," he says.

He gobbles all the cookies,
then moves on to the cheese.

He never once says *thank you!*
And he never once says *please!*

Then he calls out for his servant, and drawls, "I do believe,
I've seen enough. It's dull here. It's time for me to leave."

"I can cross you off my list.
You'll **never** win the prize.
Your town is far from perfect –
and there are fish bones in your pies."

He strides back to his boat.
He gives a little wave.

The rockhoppers are teary. The chinstraps start to cry.

But a little penguin smiles
as the Emperor sails away.
"I think the Emperor's taught us
that it's time to change our ways..."

"Manners are important.
All this time we have been blind.
Saying *please* and *thank you* –
it's a way of being **kind**."
Politeness makes a difference,
and it doesn't cost a thing.
Everyone should try it...
...from a gentoo...
...to a king!

So the penguins all decided, that from now on they would be...
the **POLITEST, KINDEST PENGUINS**, the world had ever seen!

As for the haughty Emperor,
will he change his **attitude**?
Will anyone dare say to him…

You're really
VERY RUDE!
MISS MOLLY'S SCHOOL OF MANNERS